LAND OF LÖTS

Written by Christian Carl
& Illustrated by Joyce Fan
With Chuck & Sue Willis

AuthorHouse™
1663 Liberty Drive
Bloomington, IN 47403
www.authorhouse.com
Phone: 833-262-8899

Because of the dynamic nature of the Internet, any web addresses or links contained in this book may have changed
since publication and may no longer be valid. The views expressed in this work are solely those of the author and do
not necessarily reflect the views of the publisher, and the publisher hereby disclaims any responsibility for them.

This book is printed on acid-free paper.

ISBN: 978-1-6655-2577-0 (sc)
ISBN: 978-1-6655-2576-3 (hc)
ISBN: 978-1-6655-2578-7 (e)

Library of Congress Control Number: 2021909850

Printed in China.

Published by AuthorHouse 07/31/2021

authorHOUSE

LAND OF LOTS

Written by Christian Carl
& Illustrated by Joyce Fan
With Chuck & Sue Willis

Lovelot was just a girl roaming through space.

Till she came upon a strange and magical place.

She decided to take a closer look.

And so begins our very first book.

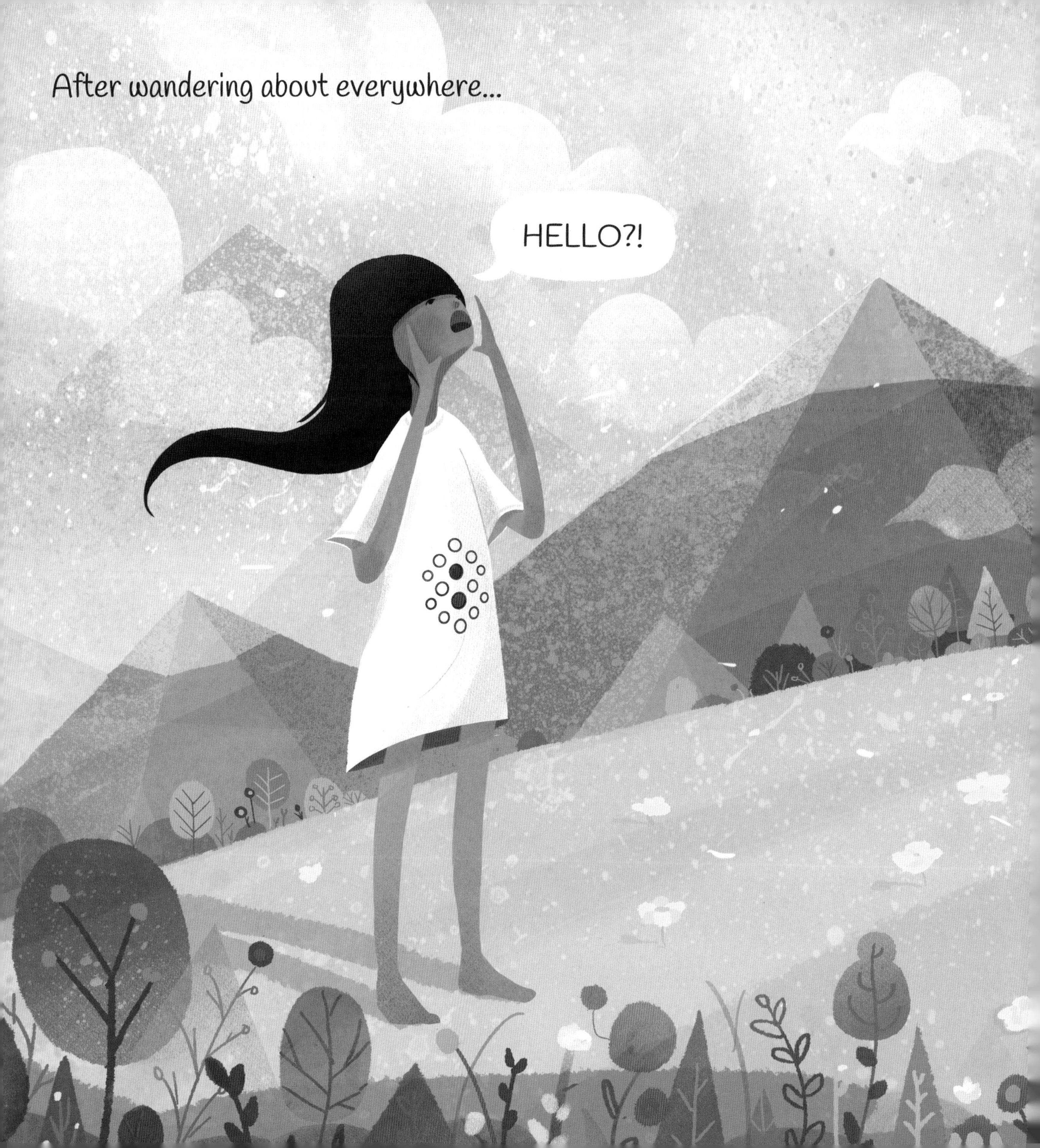
After wandering about everywhere...
HELLO?!

She discovered the Oomlots who lived there.

It was awkward at first and no one knew what to say.

Then Lovelot broke the ice with a casual hey.

She thought getting to know them could be fun.

And she quickly grew to love every single one.

She loved Cubby because he loved to hug lots.
Even though he held her too tight and wouldn't let go.

She loved Rory because he loved to roar lots.
Even though he couldn't remember to keep his voice low.

She loved Paige because she loved to read lots.
Even though she was an uncomfortably clever girl.

She loved Foggy because he loved to daydream lots.
Even though he was lost in his own little world.

She loved Peggy because she loved to cook lots.
Even though she couldn't help but make a mess.

She loved Bucky because he loved to build lots.
Even though it wouldn't be wrong to call him careless.

She loved Rainy because she loved to garden lots.
Even though leaping before she looked often got her into trouble.

She loved Gill because he loved to talk lots.
Even though his tales were so tall he needed a bigger speech bubble.

She loved Janie because she loved to explore lots.
Even though she could be a little bit too daring.

DID YOU HAVE TO STICK YOUR NECK INTO THAT CAVE?

ADVENTURE WAS CALLING!!!!
ARE WE PLAYING TAG? AM I IT?

She loved Penny because she loved to knit lots.
Even though she wasn't a big fan of sharing.

She loved Dewey because he loved to help lots.
Even though he helped himself more than he cared to admit.

She loved Rudy because he loved to laugh lots.
Even though he could go from happy to sad lickety-split.

That night Lovelot went back to her ship looking a little weary.

And dreamt of how peaceful her life in space used to be.

The next morning she woke up to a big Cubby grin.

He had a surprise for her and all the Oomlots pitched in.

A house painted purple with stars! Let the adventures begin.

Cubby loves to hug lots.

Penny loves to knit lots.

Paige loves to read lots.

Rainy loves to garden lots.

Janie loves to explore lots.

Foggy loves to daydream lots.

ewey loves to help lots.

SO MANY ARMS, SO LITTLE TIME.

Bucky loves to build lots.

NAILED IT!

dy loves to laugh lots.

WELL, TICKLE MY FEATHERS!

Rory loves to roar lots.

LOUD IS THE ONLY WAY TO LIVE.

l loves to talk lots.

HONEST TO COD, I CAN'T SWIM.

Peggy loves to cook lots.

WHIP IT GOOD!

ABOUT THE CREATORS

Christian Carl

I've helped raise three kids ages 27, 17 and six. Though the world has changed a lot over nearly three decades of parenthood—one thing hasn't. Kids are impetuous, impatient, obsessive, selfish, clingy, loud, careless, moody, imaginative, loving, caring, beautiful, and oddly smart little beings who just need two things from us – patience and a plan. Land of Lots is a faraway planet, but it hits close to home for me. And I hope it does for you too.

Joyce Fan

A Hong Kong born, Portland Oregon raised artist. Her illustrative work is often reminiscent of her childhood imaginations and its whimsical adventures. Art, food, toys and music are among the many things that keep her creative juices flowing.

Chuck and Sue Willis

Together they have been in film and advertising collectively for over half a century and working with author Christian Carl on Land of Lots for what seems like a millennium. They hope the books bring you lots of laughs, learning and love.

We'd love to hear from you!
info@thelandoflots.com
www.thelandoflots.com